SHARE A STORY

The Old Woman and the Red Pumpkin

Introduction

One of the best ways you can help
your children learn and learn to read
is to share books with them. Here's why:

• They get to know the **sounds**, **rhythms** and **words**
used in the way we write. This is different from how we
talk, so hearing stories helps children learn how to read.

• They think about the **feelings** of the characters
in the book. This helps them as they go about
their own lives with other people.

• They think about the **ideas** in the book. This helps
them to understand the world.

• Sharing books and listening to what your children
say about them shows your children that you care
about them, you care about what they think
and who they are.

Michael Rosen

Michael Rosen
Writer and Poet
Children's Laureate (2007-9)

For Joyce Biswas and Helen and Herbert Gordon
B.B.

For Nanna Leather
R.M.

First published 1998 by Walker Books Ltd
87 Vauxhall Walk, London SE11 5HJ

This edition published 2011

2 4 6 8 10 9 7 5 3 1

Text © 1975, 1998 Betsy Bang
Illustrations © 1998 Rachel Merriman
Concluding notes © CLPE 2011

This book has been typeset in Frutiger Light

Printed in China

British Library Cataloguing in Publication Data:
a catalogue record for this book is available from the British Library

ISBN 978-1-4063-3514-9

www.walker.co.uk

The Old Woman and the Red Pumpkin

A Bengali folk tale

translated and adapted by
Betsy Bang

Illustrated by
Rachel Merriman

WALKER BOOKS
AND SUBSIDIARIES
LONDON • BOSTON • SYDNEY • AUCKLAND

There was once an old woman
who was so bent over she had
to hold herself up with a stick,
and she waggled her head
when she walked, tok-tok.

One day she set out
to visit her granddaughter.
She left her house, walked through
the markets, past the river and
into the deep, dark forest.

She had gone only a little way into the forest
when a jackal suddenly jumped out from behind a tree.
"Ury bop! An old woman!" it cried. "Old woman,
I'm going to eat you up!"

"Wait!" she said. "Eat me now, and what will you get but skin and bones? I'm on my way to my granddaughter's house, and there I'll grow round and fat."

"Ach-cha," said the jackal. "Go and get fat, and when you come back, I'll eat you."

The old woman went on her way, leaning on her stick and wagging her head, tok-tok.

A little further on, a tiger
jumped out from behind a tree.
"Ury bop! An old woman!" it said.
"Old woman, I'm going to eat you up!"

"Wait!" she cried. "Eat me now, and what will you get but skin and bones? I'm on my way to my granddaughter's house, and there I'll grow round and fat."

"Ach-cha," said the tiger. "Go and get fat, and when you come back, I'll eat you."

So the old woman went on her way, leaning on her stick and wagging her head, tok-tok.

She had almost reached her granddaughter's
house, when suddenly out jumped a bear.
"Ury bop! An old woman!" it said.
"Old woman, I'm going to eat you up!"

"Wait!" she said. "Eat me now, and what will you get but skin and bones? I'm on my way to my granddaughter's house, and there I'll grow round and fat."

"Ach-cha," said the bear. "Go and get fat, and when you come back, I'll eat you."

When the old woman got to her granddaughter's house,
she ate curds and curry and curry and curds
and curds and curry and more.
And how fat she got! A little fatter and she would have burst.

"Dear granddaughter, I must go back home now," she said.

"But I'm so fat I can't walk any more. I'll have to go in a cart.

A bear and a tiger and a jackal are waiting on the road to eat me up.

Ah, me! I don't know what to do!"

"Don't worry, Deedeema," said her granddaughter.
"I'll put you inside this red pumpkin shell,
and the bear and the tiger and the jackal
won't know you're there."

She put the old woman into the pumpkin shell,
along with some tamarinds, plums and rice,
so she would have something to eat.

"Hey-yo!" She gave the pumpkin a push and
it started rolling down the road.

The pumpkin rolled and the
pumpkin rolled, and the old woman
inside began to sing,

"Pumpkin, pumpkin, roll along.
I eat tamarinds, I do.
I eat plums and rice, I do,
While I sing my song."

Now who was waiting in the
middle of the road but the bear,
who drooled as he thought of the
fat old woman he was going to eat.
The bear saw the red pumpkin come
rolling down the road and heard
a voice from inside singing.
But the bear only snorted and gave
the pumpkin a push with his paw,
and it went rolling on down the road.

"What a strange singing pumpkin,"
the bear said to himself as he watched it
roll away. He turned and followed after it,
and inside the old woman sang,

"Pumpkin, pumpkin, roll along.
I eat tamarinds, I do.
I eat plums and rice, I do,
While I sing my song."

A little further on, the tiger
was waiting in the middle of
the road, drooling as he thought
of the fat old woman
he was going to eat.
The tiger saw the red pumpkin come
rolling along and heard a voice
from inside singing.
The tiger growled and gave it
a push with his paw, and
the pumpkin rolled on down
the road, with the bear
trotting behind it.

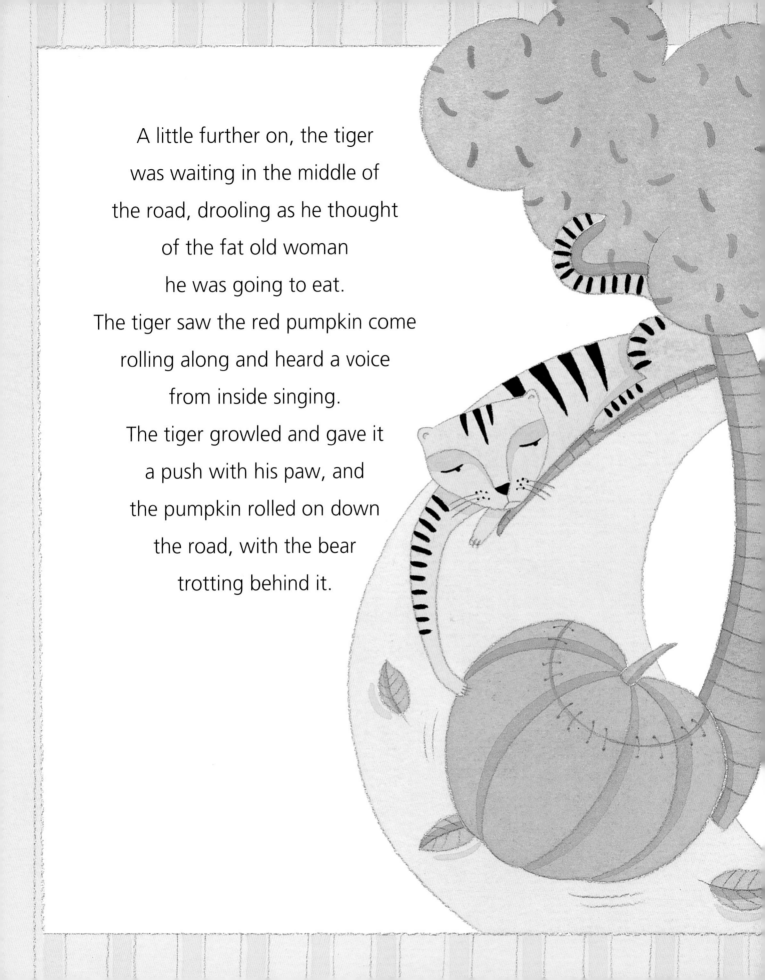

"But what a strange singing red
pumpkin with a bear behind it,"
the tiger said to himself, and he
trotted along with the bear,
while from inside the
old woman sang,

"Pumpkin, pumpkin, roll along.
I eat tamarinds, I do.
I eat plums and rice, I do,
While I sing my song."

Still further on, the jackal was waiting in the middle of the road.
When the jackal saw the pumpkin come rolling along
and heard the voice from inside singing, he jumped up.
"Ho! What's a pumpkin doing singing?" he cried.
The jackal hit the red pumpkin with a stick and broke it open,
and out popped the old woman.

"Old woman, I'll eat you up," said the jackal.

The bear came running up. "Old woman,

I'll eat you up," he said.

The tiger came running too. "Old woman, I'll eat you up," he said.

"Of course you will," the old woman replied,

"and the strongest of you should have my head."

"I'm strongest!"
cried the bear.

"I'm strongest!"
cried the tiger, and he
grabbed the bear
by the neck.

"I'm strongest!"
cried the jackal,
and he bit the
tiger's tail.

The bear growled,
the tiger roared and
the jackal howled.
What a snarling and biting
and pulling there was!

And while they were fighting,
the fat old woman
crept away …

and ran
until she got
safely home.

Sharing Stories

Sharing stories together is a pleasurable way
to help children learn to read and enjoy books.
Reading stories aloud and encouraging
children to talk about the pictures and join in
with parts of the story they know well are
good ways to build their interest in books.
They will want to share their favourite books
again and again. This is an important part
of becoming a successful reader.

The Old Woman and the Red Pumpkin is a new telling of a traditional Indian folk tale about a brave grandmother who outwits the wild animals in the forest to get safely home. Here are some ways you can share this book:

• Read and re-read the book and talk about the illustrations together to deepen children's experience of a different time and place in this special "story world".

• There are lots of patterns in this book to help children remember the story and join in. For example you could point out the pattern of three animals and the repeated phrases which help them predict what comes next.

• Once they know the book well, encourage children to read it for themselves. When they get stuck on a word you can help them to make a good guess by pointing at the pictures, or reading on to the end of a sentence and asking them what would make sense. Praise good guesses even if they don't match word for word what's in the book. Readers need the confidence to take risks.

• Together you can draw a picture-map of the grandmother's journey. Start from her house and use the story and pictures to guide you, drawing and labelling the places she passes and the animals she meets on the way to and from her granddaughter's house.

• This is a good story to tell. Children can use their picture-map to tell the story in their own words.

SHARE A STORY
A First Reading Programme
From Pre-school to School

Beginnings – 2 years+

Early Steps – 3 years+

Next Steps – 4 years+

Taking Off – 5 years+

Sharing the best books makes the best readers

WALKER BOOKS

www.walker.co.uk